Weather Wear

Dona Herweck Rice

Publishing Credits

Rachelle Cracchiolo, M.S.Ed., *Publisher*
Conni Medina, M.A.Ed., *Managing Editor*
Nika Fabienke, Ed.D., *Content Director*
Véronique Bos, *Creative Director*
Shaun N. Bernadou, *Art Director*
Valerie Morales, *Associate Editor*
John Leach, *Assistant Editor*
Courtney Roberson, *Senior Graphic Designer*

Image Credits: p.9 (top) Christine Langer-Püschel/Dreamstime; all other images from iStock and/or Shutterstock.

Library of Congress Cataloging-in-Publication Data

Names: Rice, Dona, author.
Title: Weather wear / Dona Herweck Rice.
Description: Huntington Beach, CA : Teacher Created Materials, [2019] | Audience: K to grade 3. |
Identifiers: LCCN 2018029755 (print) | LCCN 2018031395 (ebook) | ISBN 9781493899180 | ISBN 9781493898442
Subjects: LCSH: Clothing and dress--Juvenile literature. | Weather--Juvenile literature. | Vocabulary.
Classification: LCC GT518 (ebook) | LCC GT518 .R527 2019 (print) | DDC 391.4/8--dc23
LC record available at https://lccn.loc.gov/2018029755

Teacher Created Materials
5301 Oceanus Drive
Huntington Beach, CA 92649-1030
www.tcmpub.com

ISBN 978-1-4938-9844-2

Printed in China
Nordica.082018.CA21800936

I0895253

"There is a time for

 ," she said.

mittens

"There is a time for

bathing suits

," she said.

"There is a time for

,” she said.

scarves

"There is a time for

shorts

," she said.

"There is a time for

,” she said.

boots

"There is a time for

 ," she said.

sundresses

"There is a time for

hats

," she said.

"There is a time for

," she said.

sunglasses

"There is a time for

,"she said.

coats

"There is a time for

,"
she said.

sandals

High-Frequency Words

New Words

said she
there time

Review Words

a for
is